Will I See You Today?

Written by Crystal Bowman
and Ava Pennington

Illustrated by Dan Dunham

Standard®
PUBLISHING

Cincinnati, Ohio

Published by Standard Publishing, Cincinnati, Ohio
www.standardpub.com

Also available: *Do You Love Me More?* ISBN 978-0-7847-2916-8, Copyright © 2011 by Standard Publishing.

Printed in: China
Project editor: Elaina Meyers
Illustrator: Dan Dunham
Cover & interior design: Sandra S. Wimmer

ISBN 978-0-7847-2917-5

Library of Congress Cataloging-in-Publication Data

Library of Congress Cataloging-in-Publication Data

Bowman, Crystal.
  Will I see You today? / written by Crystal Bowman and Ava Pennington ; illustrated by Dan Dunham.
    p. cm.
  ISBN 978-0-7847-2917-5 (casebound)
  1. God--Christianity--Juvenile literature. 2. Revelation--Christianity--Juvenile literature. I. Pennington, Ava, 1958- II. Dunham, Dan. III. Title.
  BT107.B69 2010
  231.7--dc22
                          2010036591

16 15 14 13 12 11   1 2 3 4 5 6 7 8 9

From Crystal
   To my MOPS moms who help their little ones see God.

From Ava
   To the memory of Aunt Ramona—the first person to tell me the stories of Jesus.

From Dan
   For Bethany.

I look into the big blue sky, and God, I know you're there.

I see the things that you have made—
I see them everywhere!

I know you made the sun and moon,
to shine up in the sky.

You even made the tiny stars
that twinkle way up high.

I know you made the puffy clouds that send the rain and snow.

But God, I have a question,
and I really need to know. . .

When I go out to play will I see
you today?

You made the mighty oceans
and the mountains standing tall.

The forests and the rivers too—
I know you made them all.

The birds sing happy songs to you;
I see them in the tree.

I see your pretty flowers,
but it's you I want to see.

I know you're with me all the time no matter where I go.

But God, I have a question, and I really need to know. . .

LIBRARY

When I go out to play will I see you today?

My Bible says that long ago,
you sent your Son to earth.

An angel told the shepherds
of Jesus' special birth.

When Jesus grew to be a man,
he healed the sick and lame.

He made blind people see again and did it in your name.

He calmed the windy, stormy sea.
Then many people knew

that when they looked at Jesus
they were really seeing you.

He died upon a wooden cross
to save the world from sin.

But since he was the Son of God
he came to life again.

He went back up to Heaven—
the Bible says it's true.

And everyone who trusts in him
will go to Heaven too.

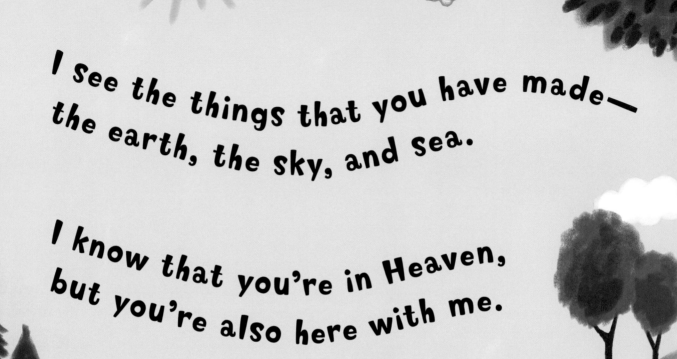

I see the things that you have made—
the earth, the sky, and sea.

I know that you're in Heaven,
but you're also here with me.

The Bible says that Heaven is a very special place.

And someday when I'm playing there, I'll see you face to face.

A Note to Parents and Teachers

Young children process much of their information through experiences and concrete images. Therefore, while your children may be confident that God exists, they may struggle with the fact that he is an invisible Spirit.

Scripture explains that God reveals himself in two main ways. The first way is called general revelation, and it means that God reveals himself in the natural world around us. The Bible describes general revelation in the following verses:

Psalm 19:1-3 "The heavens tell about the glory of God. The skies show that his hands created them. Day after day they speak about it. Night after night they make it known. But they don't speak or use words. No sound is heard from them."

Romans 1:20 "Ever since the world was created it has been possible to see the qualities of God that are not seen. I'm talking about his eternal power and about the fact that he is God. Those things can be seen in what he has made. So people have no excuse for what they do."

The second way God reveals himself is called special revelation, and it includes how God reveals himself through his Word and through his Son, Jesus Christ. The Bible explains special revelation in these verses:

> **Hebrews 1:1-3** "In the past, God spoke to our people through the prophets. He spoke at many times. He spoke in different ways. But in these last days, he has spoken to us through his Son. He is the one whom God appointed to receive all things. God made everything through him. The Son is the gleaming brightness of God's glory. He is the exact likeness of God's being."

> **John 14:8, 9** "Philip said, 'Lord, show us the Father. That will be enough for us.' Jesus answered, 'Don't you know me, Philip? I have been among you such a long time! Anyone who has seen me has seen the Father.'"

Nature is a good starting place to show God's handiwork as proof of his existence, but we should not stop there. Children need to know that God also reveals himself through his Word and most importantly through his Son, Jesus Christ. What a wonderful way to teach our children that God is real—by pointing them to his Son, God in human form!

Jesus also assured his followers that someday we will be with him in Heaven. In John 14:2, 3, Jesus says, "I am going there to prepare a place for you. If I go and do that, I will come back. And I will take you to be with me. Then you will also be where I am."

Explain to your children that someday, all of us who believe in Jesus will see God face to face. Isn't that exciting?

Crystal Bowman is an author, speaker, and Mentor for MOPS (Mothers of Preschoolers). She has written over 60 books for children and three books for women. She also writes stories for Clubhouse Jr. Magazine and lyrics for children's piano music. Her children's books come in all shapes and sizes and many of them have become best sellers. Whether her stories are written in playful rhythm and rhyme, or short sentences for beginning readers, she tries to make them so enjoyable that kids will want to read them over and over again. "But the most important part," she says, "is to teach children that God loves them and cares about them very much." Crystal and her husband live in Florida and have three grown children.

Ava Pennington is an author, speaker, and Bible study teacher. She is the author of *One Year Alone with God: 366 Devotions on the Names of God* (Revell Books, 2010). She also writes for national magazines such as Focus on the Family's Clubhouse, Standard Publishing's The Lookout, and others. Her short stories have appeared in more than twenty anthologies, including fourteen titles in the inspirational Chicken Soup for the Soul book series. Ava has an Adult Bible Study certificate from Moody Bible Institute and teaches a weekly interdenominational Bible study class of more than 200 women. She has a heart for women's ministry, and has been a featured speaker at churches, women's groups, and community events. Ava and her husband live in Florida with their two rescue boxers.

As a young child, **Dan Dunham** drew constantly on his family's farm in Ohio. Today, he lives in the wilds of Indiana and continues to illustrate constantly, always trying to recapture the fun and expressiveness with which he drew those many years ago. This is his first picture book for Standard Publishing.